Masquerade

Jana Dibala

Masquerade

TATE PUBLISHING
AND ENTERPRISES, LLC

Published by Tate Publishing & Enterprises, LLC
127 E. Trade Center Terrace | Mustang, Oklahoma 73064 USA
1.888.361.9473 | www.tatepublishing.com

Tate Publishing is committed to excellence in the publishing industry. The company reflects the philosophy established by the founders, based on Psalm 68:11,
"The Lord gave the word and great was the company of those who published it."

Book design copyright © 2015 by Tate Publishing, LLC. All rights reserved.
Cover design by Joseph Emnace
Interior design by Jomar Ouano

Published in the United States of America

ISBN: 978-1-63449-759-6
1. Fiction / Action & Adventure
2. Fiction / Christian / Suspense
14.11.18

Introduction

With each puffing breath Karen Briscoe forced herself to run. Her feet pounded out a desperate rhythm on the asphalt with each stride.

Don't stop. Run. Faster.

She could hear her blood swishing in her ears as her heart rate increased. She felt a surge of pain shoot through her side. Her muscles wanting to cramp but the rush of adrenaline and pure survival instincts kept her running.

Looking over her right shoulder she saw no one. But she knew it was only a matter of seconds before her pursuers would be on top of her. She turned down a alley, a dead end.

No, no no!

"Check down there!" yelled a voice.

Motionless, Karen tried to form a plan. Her thoughts were clouded with the urge to go into an asthmatic attack.

Oh, no you don't! You can cough your head off later, right now you are going to breath and you going to get out of this...alive!

She saw a fire escape at the end of the alley, running towards the ladder, her body aching, she jumped into the air and grabbed the first rung. Out of pain and fear she groaned, "Lord, help me!"

Pulling herself up she was able to climb rung by rung until she was on a roof.

"I know she is here! Check everything! Now!"

Looking over the bricked ledge of her hiding place, Karen watched as three men with guns tore into dumpsters looking for her.

Breathing was becoming unbearable. Coughing would soon be inevitable.

Down in the alley there was one man not demolishing everything in sight. He looked odd standing so still. With a quick move he turned and shined his flashlight on Karen's face.

Stunned, silent, something passed between them as they starred at one another. Almost a familiarity. Then as quick as he has shined the light he turned and walked to the other men.

"I think we lost her Brett."

Brett screamed and kicked one of the bricked buildings. "Everyone in the car!"

Karen fell backwards on her back and gasped for air.

They were gone.

Chapter One

Five Years Earlier

Where is it?

Karen slammed her dresser drawer closed. She zipped her suitcase, stuffed with clothes and a few personal items.

Grabbing her purse she heard her bedroom door open. "Hey!"

Karen couldn't hide her concern as she starred at her baby sister.

They were only eighteen months apart but somehow she felt much older.

She felt like Amy's protector. And this was one of the reasons she insisted on the two of them becoming roommates while Amy studied at a local university.

With a quizzical look, Amy questioned, "Karen, what is it?"

She couldn't endanger her sister with the details of what she had been involved in or what was about to take place. All she could say was she was leaving.

"Amy, always remember I love you.

I have to go."

As Karen passed, Amy grabbed her arm. Confused and afraid, she shouted, "What are you talking about? Karen, what is going on?"

"I have made arrangements for us to be ok. You are going to have to trust me and not ask questions."

"What are you saying!" Amy shrieked. "Does this has something to with that crazed religion you have gotten yourself into!"

Karen's responded in a even tone, "Aim, I wish you could understand. What is happening is not because of my faith. I have to go. I love you."

Hot tears stung Karen's checks as she ran to her black SUV and tossed her luggage in the back seat and then sat in the driver's seat and buckled her seat belt. Driving away she began to sob.

But this is the only way. Amy has to remain safe.

Karen wanted to tell her sister everything. They only had each other. No other siblings and their parents were dead. But Amy had to have denial ability. She had spent the last year planning and preparing for this day to achieve her freedom. Freedom from the Alliance.

The day would come that she would take the Alliance down but for now escape was essential. Karen would go somewhere she would never be expected to go.

She decided on Oregon.

Present Day

Now with the Alliance catching up with her after five years of successful hiding, Karen had to think of her next moves.

Oregon proved to be a good match for her. The beautiful Willamette Valley with it's trees and rivers was a refreshing change from the skyscrapers and city noise of New York City. She had made friends and felt almost normal.

Relying on her Alliance training, Karen had planned for this day. The day when Brett, the Alliance's lead agent and head of agent training would find her.

They must be getting desperate if they have sent Brett.

Karen had chosen Oregon as her hide-a-way for several reasons. One of them being there is a tremendous amount of forest and rough terrain within the state. Perfect to get off the grid and make a successful escape route.

Now she had to get to what she called "ground zero." A place where she hid money, passports, weapons and other essential survival items.

She had found an abandoned log cabin a few miles north of the Mackenzie River and this is where her stragedy would begin.

Karen walked to a local bus stop and waited for the next scheduled bus. She would ride to the outskirts of town and from there she would hike to the cabin.

Once in route fatigue was beginning to set in.

Keep it together a little longer.

For a few minutes Karen allowed her thoughts to drift into the past. Something she rarely did.

The Alliance. It sounds so, professional. I thought I was doing something of value. Saving the world.

Right out of high school Karen was accepted in a prestigious college.

Amy was still at home, her parents, alive. Tears began to fill her eyes but she refused to let them fall.

She had been approached by a professor for a job opportunity while in college. He told her once she had a degree she had a job waiting for her with The Alliance.

Once recruited she was filled with propaganda of standards and policies for which The Alliance stood. A non-profit organization that did hundreds of charity events. From environmental awareness to raising money for orphaned children in foreign countries.

It wasn't until Karen had sat behind a desk for one full year that she received her first assignment and her first meeting with Judson Steiner.

Judson was cool, collected. A man in his late 40s. When he entered the room you felt a presence. It would not be until years later that Karen would recognize that presence as evil.

She was nervous at this first meeting but Mr. Steiner made her feel relaxed.

Judson was looking over paper work when Karen entered his office.

"You wanted to see me sir?"

He smiled a smile that was warm yet revealed nothing. "Yes, Ms. Brisoce. Please have a seat."

"Thank you."

Since this was the first time Karen met Judson she subtly analyzed him. He was not wearing a wedding band, and so she assumed he was single. But he was very attractive and obviously wealthy and powerful, so she assumed he had plenty of lady admirers.

He had a distinguished look about him. He looked middle-aged and it suited him. She could easily see he was charming. Karen decided she should wait to form an opinion on her boss.

She did a quick evaluation of Mr. Steiner's office. It was luxurious but not extravagant. If someone was knowledgeable about history then that person would know after examining the antiquities in the room that he was a historian. He owned several rare and expensive historical artifacts. Most people would have been impressed. Karen was not.

She herself a student of history, felt that Steiner having such a collection was boasting about his wealth. The pieces he had purchased were not cheap and in Karen's opinion belonged in museums.

"Do you like history?" quizzed Judson.

"Pardon me?"

"I noticed you observing my collection."

Karen embarrassed tried to think of a respectful reply.

"Oh, Ms.Briscoe don't be alarmed. You were very discreet in your observations. I being the president of this company am trained to read people and their reactions.

This comment made Karen even more embarrassed as she had just moments ago been analyzing Judson as a person. She hoped he didn't notice and if he did that he wouldn't mention it.

Judson felt Karen's tension and changed the subject.

"Ms. Briscoe, do you know why you are here?"

Relieved that Judson Steiner asked the question instead of further quizzing, Karen answered, "No, sir."

Judson folded his hands and leaned back in his chair.

"I have been watching you. You signed with us a year ago, correct?"

"That is correct."

"You are an exemplary employee.

You graduated top of your class. And while working here, you are punctual, efficient and your co- workers have all given you glowing reports."

But there is quite a bit more that makes you special."

Karen sat quietly, waiting for Mr. Steiner to continue.

"You see, I think you are the type of person that can be trained, no molded into an agent."

"Agent, sir?"

"Yes." Now Judson was standing, hands behind his back as he paced the floor.

"You see, very few people know that The Alliance has a division of agents. Men and women that work a unique side of The Alliance."

"People of service, one might say."

"Service for what, sir?"

"A tremendous amount of things.

"Mainly, we don't want anyone to stand in our way of progress. No matter how great or small." Karen's mind was now back to the present as she felt a jolt. The bus had stopped. The sun was setting. She would have to hurry if she would make it to the log cabin by night fall.

She hiked at a quick pace but did not push herself. She knew that energy and stamina was something she would need in the days ahead.

Once at the cabin she did a quick investigation, making certain nothing had been tampered with and that she was safe. Affirming that everything was as it should be Karen pulled a fire-proof lock box and duffel bag out from under the wood plank on the floor. In the bag she had a change of clothes and shoes, a wig, and colored contacts, a make-up bag along with bottles of water and trail mix. In the box was money passports, a gun and most importantly documents.

Opening the box, Karen pulled out a micro-chip. This was the real reason The Alliance wanted her dead. The threat of exposure.

Sure, she was a liability, but on this secure digital chip was the dark secrets that The Alliance buried within it's walls. Bribes, mob-connections and murder.

The right connection and the right timing, Karen would expose The Alliance. After that she possibly could have a normal life. For now, survival and exposure was all Karen could think about. After moving all the items from the lock box into the duffel bag she was ready to move on.

But first,she would need rest. She decided to spend the night at the cabin. Sleep came quickly but also restless. Nightmares plagued her into the wee hours of the morning. She woke with a start at the sound of a twig snapping outside.

The cabin was dark, the only light illuminating it's rustic interior was the moonlight trickling through the window.

She eyed her gun across the cabin floor. A lazy mistake not having it on her at all times.

Time was of the essence as she heard footsteps nearing the front door. Not confident that she could get her weapon before her attacker was on her, Karen grabbed her make-up bag that was in her duffel bag lying next to her.

Something she had put together herself and carried on many assignments. To an innocent eye it was a small make up bag. Inside was one lipstick, a bottle of perfume and a compact mirror.

But in actuality these were weapons more deadly than even her gun. Part of the danger lied in the close contact they required to be used. The bottom of the lipstick contained a extremely small but lethal syringe. It was filled with a chemical that would paralyze it's victim for three minutes. Her perfume was a toxic spray that would knock out a three-hundred-pound man for ten minutes. And the compact mirror contained truth serum.

Now with the chemical syringe in hand Karen hid behind the door ready to pounce on her prey.

Slowly, the door creaked. She didn't hesitate. She stabbed the syringe in the man's neck as he fell to the ground.

Karen was like a machine. She moved step by step through the training she had received from The Alliance to take out a target.

While her pursuer was passed out on the floor, Karen flipped open the compact mirror. One side was an ordinary mirror, on the other side was a small vial. This was the truth serum. Karen opened it and poured the into the man's mouth.

She dragged him over to a wood post that was in the center of the room. There she propped him up and tied his hands and feet to the post with some rope she had hidden inside the cabin.

Moments passed. He squinted his eyes open, trying to recall what happened. He wiggled a bit, then realized he was tied up. He blankly stared at Karen.

"Who are you?" She questioned coolly.

No answer.

She paced the floor trying to figure out what questions would push him to answer her. With the serum in effect, if he answered, his replies would be truthful. But being well trained by The Alliance he may not answer at all.

Karen squatted and looked him in the eyes. "You were the one in the alley. You saw me but didn't turn me over to Brett. Why?"

"We are on the same side." he replied with a raspy voice. "What did you do to me?"

"I drugged you and you should be thankful you are even alive." Karen replied matter-of-factly.

The man's head ducked down. His brain felt like it would pound out of his skull. Karen's voice was even and calm but to him it sounded like a crash of cymbals.

"Could you stop yelling."

"First, who are you?"

"My name is Mario Valdez. I am an agent with The Alliance and like you I went rouge."

Cautiously, Karen challenged, "If you are rouge then how are you still working for The Alliance?"

"I am a double agent. Well, I was a double agent. A few hours ago I suspected that I was being made and I decided to find you and help you."

Karen eyed him carefully.

"You know I can't lie. If you have followed your training then you have truth serum, or powder, or something like that around here. I am sure you gave it to me, so you know I am telling the truth."

Still suspicious Karen wasn't sure how to process what Mario was saying.

What if there was some counter-measure to the truth serum that I was never told about.

"So why are you helping me?"

"Untie me and I will answer all your questions, but not here and not now. They are closing in on you and it is only a matter of time before they find this place. I have a car about a mile from here. We leave now, get on the road and plan our next move."

Like it or not, Karen was going to have to trust him. She was fortunate that the cabin remained a safe-house for as long as it did. But now with Mario gone, Brett would be even more fierce in his search.

"Fine. Be still." Karen cut Mario's ties. He stood. "Let's go."

Chapter Two

Fifteen Years Earlier

"Stop! Police!"

Mario ran down a narrow alley way, looking over his shoulder.

Dead end. No!

The rushing footsteps of two uniformed cops drew closer behind Mario.

"Freeze! Hands in the air!"

Mario did as he was told and the tall, lanky police officer grabbed his wrists and cuffed them with handcuffs.

"So, you think it is fun to run from the police. Let's see how much fun you have in a jail cell."

After a twenty minute car ride in the back of the police car, Mario was sitting in the police station in a small room with a mirror to his right. He had been here before. A troubled teen, belonging to a gang, he had been arrested several times for theft, vandalism and under aged drinking.

But today he wasn't a teenager, he was a twenty-five years old man with a juvenile record and two strikes against him as an adult. This time he was headed for the state penitentiary.

A man in a dark gray suit came in to the room. He sat down in the chair across from Mario.

"Do you know what kind of trouble you are in?"

Mario smirked. *Cops, they always think they can scare you.*

"Well, maybe you don't. But I am here to give you a way out."

This caught his attention. Even though he put up a tough front, he didn't want to go to prison.

"What do you mean by a way out."

"Well, I have a company. Right now it is slightly small but one day we will be global."

"What does that have to do with me."

The man frowned. "Patience. We will have to work on that. If you accept my job offer."

Mario, skeptical, asked, "What job?"

"You see Mr. Valdez, even though my company is small, we have influential friends in high-ranking places. Come and work for me and your record, all of your record is wiped clean. No jail time."

"What is the catch?"

"No catch. I need team members like you. A quality of people that can get things done quickly and with no mess."

"I don't know man. You sound good but I grew up in the streets, bro, there is always a price."

"It is up to you Mr. Valdez. This is a legitimate business contract."

"I want someone of your caliber to do my business. This is a regular, honest job. You do the work you get paid, handsomely. Also, as you progress in the company your wages and benefits will grow with you."

Then the man smiled a sly smile,

"And no jail time, bro."

Mario stared at the man for a few moments. He was leery but he didn't want to go to jail.

"Ok, you have a deal."

"Great! I look forward to working together. A car will pick you up at your house tomorrow morning, 8:00am sharp."

The man turned to leave when Mario called out, "Hey! I never caught your name."

Again with the same smile, the man replied, "How rude of me, I am Judson Steiner."

The next day just as Judson had said, there was a car waiting for Mario outside of his apartment.

It wasn't until he was inside the plush New York business building and seated at his desk that he thought, *Not bad for a kid from the Bronx.*

"Hey there."

Startled, Mario looked up to see Brett Stevens standing over his desk.

"Oh, hey."

Brett stuck out his hand, Mario shook it and then replied, "This is my first day."

"I know. I have been assigned to be your trainer. So, if you will follow me, I will show you the gym and we will get started."

"Ok." Mario followed Brett into the elevator. "I do have one question."

"Sure."

"Judson, I mean Mr. Steiner, said his company was small. I am confused. I mean look at this place. It is massive. And it has it's own gym?"

Brett laughed hardily. "Yeah, that sounds like Judson alright. He is a visionary. Because we are not global, we are small. At least that is what he thinks."

"Oh, ok. Another question. What kind of work will I be doing?"

"You ask a lot of questions. That's good."

Brett slapped Mario on the back. "All questions will be answered in good time."

Once in the gym Brett and Mario put in a strenuous work out. And they did so every day for six months.

Mario became so obsessed with the work, he did extra hours in the gym on his own, sometimes even sleeping at the office.

Chapter Three

Inside Mr. Steiner's office Brett sat in a taupe, wing back chair.

"What do you think? Is he ready?"

"He's ready."

Judson had been looking out the window, admiring the exquisite New York view and then turned to face Brett.

"You are sure?"

Brett leaned forward a few inches and locked eyes with Judson. "He is ready."

"Good, good." Judson replied, turning to face the New York skyline again. "There is a file on my desk, take it and give it to him. This will be his first assignment."

Brett picked up the file and left Judson's office.

Alone, Judson said to himself, "Now it begins."

Heading to the gym with the paperwork in hand Brett ran into Mario as he was leaving.

"There you are. I thought you forgot about me." Mario teased.

"I have something for you."

Curious, Mario opened the file and thumbed through the papers.

"What is this?"

"Your first assignment."

Mario smiled a beaming smile.

"Really? You aren't pulling some kind of prank are you?"

Brett couldn't help but grin. "No prank. Your first assignment."

Mario laughed loudly and hugged Brett. "Woo! Yes!"

Brett knowing that Mario had a boisterous personality took it all in stride."

"Thanks, man. I really appreciate all you have done for me."

Brett now more reserved, replied, "Not a problem. It is my job. Now you best go to your desk, review the files and get yourself acquainted with the ins and outs of this assignment. You will be on a plane at 0:900 hours."

At his desk, Mario opened the file. The first few papers were informative. The description was that the target was a young woman named Jaden Oliver. *Target? That is a funny term to use.*

She was a senator's wife and she had been unfaithful to him. Not only that, she was also working with the very senator that was running against her husband in the upcoming election. She was to be eliminated.

Eliminated?

Mario stood in front of Brett's desk, where he dropped the file.

"I can't do this."

Brett folded his hands together and leaned back in his chair. His green eyes were vibrant. For a moment he said nothing.

When he did finally speak he said, "What do you mean you can't do it? That is what we have been training for."

"Whoa, whoa, whoa! I am not a murdered!" Mario shouted while he paced frantically around Brett's office.

"And just what do you mean, this is what we have been training for? I never signed on for this!"

Now Brett stood with both hands on his desk and leaned intently over for emphasis. "Oh yes you did! And you will do this assignment. Or have you forgotten all that Mr. Steiner has done for you?"

"I don't care! I will go to prison before I do this! I am a lot of things but I am no killer!"

Now Brett was nose to nose with Mario. He was calm but methodical.

"You will do the assignment, Mario. Or have you forgotten how The Alliance has taken care of your mother and sister? Brett paused.

"How are they by the way?"

Mario clenched his fist. "You hurt them and I swear…"

"Do the assignment and all things will be as they should be. Your mom and sister will remain safe. After all, we protect our own."

Mario was speechless.

He thought, *I knew there was a price.*

That night he barely slept. The next day he was on the plane, as was Brett. The day went quickly. He was given a small vial. All he had to do was pretend to be a waiter at Mrs.Oliver's favorite coffee shop. He was to slip the poison in her drink and he was done. And he did it. Quietly and quickly.

That night back at his lavish home, that he could now afford thanks to his position at The Alliance, he stood in his shower letting the spray of water trickle down his back. He grabbed the soap and started scrubbing his hands,scrubbing and scrubbing.

Rubbing them raw in the hopes of cleaning off the evil he had done.

But it was of no use. He was now changed. He had killed someone and he was now an agent of The Alliance.

Chapter Four

Present Day

Once in Mario's Ford pick-up, Karen started quizzing.

"Start talking."

"It's a nice night."

"Very funny. What made you decide to leave The Alliance? And why and how did you find me?" Karen was even more concerned about Mario's answers. The truth serum had worn off by now. She knew he was rouge and that he was wanted by The Alliance. That bit of knowledge comforted her. But whatever he said from now on she would have to question.

"Why did you leave The Alliance?" Mario questioned.

Karen remembered a particular day that was going to change who she was and change her life forever.

"We aren't talking about me!"

"We should be." Mario grinned at her from the driver's seat. "We are going to have to trust each other."

Karen felt anger welling up inside of her. *Who does he think he is! I was doing just fine without him. He is so calm and smug.*

"Trust is earned." She replied flatly.

"Ok, I will try to earn your trust." Mario said.

"You could start by telling me how you came to the decision to leave The Alliance." Karen replied.

"That isn't a choice easily made, as you know. Some say there is no choice in the matter." Mario stopped. His eyes seemed distant, like in another place. Then he said quietly, "I guess, I just couldn't target people anymore."

Karen was careful with her words, she wanted to remain collected.

"What case changed it for you?"

"A single mom." Mario almost whispered. Karen knew this wasn't a ploy but his real reason for leaving The Alliance.

"It is strange. I had hundreds of assignments. Most of them dealing with women. Sometimes to get to their important husband, sometimes they themselves were to be taken out. They became like animals to me. I couldn't look at them as a person. They were an assignment."

Karen knew this feeling.

"For some reason this mom got to me."

"Why was she targeted?"

"She organized various charities and some of them were for religious based organizations. The Alliance, wanting to keep up their reputation, offered to put her in charge of one of their charities. She turned them down. I don't know what she knew about The Alliance or if she knew anything at all. But that doesn't matter. Just the possibility that she could be a liability was enough to target her. So I was given the assignment."

"Something about her. She had this peace. Something I never had. I just couldn't do it. So I scared her and told her to get out of town and never return. I lied to The Alliance and reported that she had already skipped town once I went to do the job."

Mario's expression saddened, "I can't help but feel like I had a part in her death."

"They caught up with her didn't they." Karen questioned.

"Yes, it was then I realized it didn't matter what I did or said, The Alliance would win. So, I knew that I couldn't be done, just in a snap. So I started working from the inside."

"A double agent."

"Yes. I wasn't sure how I was going to go about it all at first.

But as time went on, I thought, there has to be more like me.

Other agents wanting out but trapped."

Mario's words cut Karen like a knife. It was all too real. The same feelings he had were the same as her own.

She wanted to open up to him but she couldn't bring herself to fully trust him. Maybe one day she could but for now she kept her secrets.

She needed a different topic.

"Where are we going?"

"Texas. I have connections there."

"Texas is one of the few places I have not been. I have wanted to go, so I guess this is as good of a time as any."

Mario smiled, a little surprised at Karen's optimism. He wanted to know more about her. But he knew if he pushed she would pull further away.

The highway miles stretched before them and little was spoken.

Karen, exhausted and coming down from an adrenaline high, drifted into sleep. She soon awoke with a jolt, as Mario parked the truck.

"Where are we?" She asked while rubbing her eyes.

"Laramie, Wyoming."

Karen noticed the neon flashes of a vacancy sign. "We are stopping?"

"Just for a few hours rest. We need to keep up our energy."

Karen nodded and pulled the door handle, but Mario stopped her.

"Wait here." he said. "I will get us a couple of rooms."

Head back on the seat Karen shut her yes. She was thinking about her first assignment. Brett had trained her and he thought she was ready.

"All you have to do is slip this poison into his drink. We will handle the rest. Karen, worried, replied, "What if I mess this up?"

Brett laughed, "You can't mess this up. It is a Gala. You dress up, have fun, flirt a bit." Karen smiled.

"And when the time is right…"

Brett handed her a ruby ring. He flipped it open showing her the compartment that held the poison.

Karen placed the ring on her left index finger. "If you think I am ready, then I can do it."

"That's my girl."

Karen's mind returned to the present, she heard a tapping on the window and saw Mario standing outside her door.

"You are in room eight and I am in room nine." He handed Karen her key.

"Meet in my room in three hours. We have plans to make and we need to be together in everything."

"Three hours then." Karen answered.

Once in her small motel room, Karen laid on the bed. She was sure sleep wouldn't come easily.

Instead of trying to force rest she decided to put together a plan to present to Mario.

But Karen's mind couldn't think tactics. Her mind was focused on Mario.

I will wait and see what he wants to do. How far does he want to go with this? Does he just want to secure survival? Or does he want what I want? To take down The Alliance. Disband them. Imprison them.

The red glow from the alarm clock on the dresser showed 3:00 am. *Time to meet Mario.*

Karen grabbed her bag, put her gun in the back of her jean and walked to room nine.

Mario opened the door before she could knock.

"Sleep well?"

"Not really. Did you?"

Mario didn't answer, "Let's get to work."

On a small card table Karen saw papers, notes and sketchings.

"So what is all this?"

"Everything I can remember about The Alliance. What I have drawn up is a layout of their headquarters, all the offices, the restrooms."

"Everything. We will be able to get in through here." Mario pointed to a ventilation shaft.

Confused Karen asked, "We are going inside The Alliance? Why?"

"For information."

Still puzzled Karen waited for Mario to reveal his plan.

"What are your goals?"

"My goals? Are you asking about my hopes and dreams? Do I want to have 2.5 kids and live in Suburbia?" Karen replied sarcastically.

"Do you want to run the rest of your life? Never knowing what lurks behind every move you make. Is that what you want? Or do you want to go against The Alliance, no holds bard, take them out and make them the next target."

This is what Karen wanted to hear. She handed Mario her digital card. "On here is information about The Alliance. They could never buy their way out of what is on this."

Mario took the SD card and looked at it in the palm of his hand. He then looked at Karen.

Not only was she intelligent, brave and fiery she was also beautiful. She was tall, had a broad build but was also delicate. Karen brushed her auburn hair behind her ear.

"Your SD card is worthless."

"What do you mean?" She grabbed the card from Mario's hand and examined it. She could see no damage.

"How long were you with The Alliance?"

"Eight years, why?"

"I was with them fifteen years. Plus, I earned a spot in the agent training department directly under Brett."

"What is your point?" Karen asked.

She was getting irritated.

"Did you think you were the first agent to question The Alliance? To think you could leave them?"

"I put together a program. One that was placed on every agent's computer. A virus. If an agent went into files above their clearance or downloaded things, we knew about it. And anything that was out-sourced to any device was infected with a virus that would delete those files off of that device."

"That can't be possible! I checked, I saw the files on my SD card!"

"Yes, but are they still there?"

Mario reached into the pocket of the black vest he was wearing and pulled out a small computer.

"Let's find out."

Karen took the computer and inserted the SD card. The screen read, *files not found.*

"I have worked on those files for over a year!" Karen's chest felt tight. Anxiety pulsated through her body.

"I already know." Mario said calmly. He was now filling a glass with water for Karen. He handed it to her and continued.

"The Alliance was on to you from the start because of the virus I created. I handle the cases of agents looking at documentation that could lead to problems for Judson. So, I started tracking your computer, and covered for you. In doing this, I learned that you and I had a chance to be allies. I waited for the right time for us to work together."

"Why didn't you allow the card to keep the files?"

"Even I am not that good. That would required reprogramming the system and that would have immediately alerted The Alliance.

Karen felt a surge of pain in her chest. He asthma flared and she had to concentrate on taking even breaths.

She had depended on that documentation, as her "ace in the hole."

Now she felt helpless and defeated.

"What will we do now?"

"We go back inside The Alliance."

"You are serious?"

Mario and Karen sat across from one another, fatigued but focused. "There is one computer that doesn't not have the virus program. And that is in Judson's office."

"You are serious!"

"Very much so. This can be done and I know how to get to the files we need. With these files we can find witnesses."

"Witnesses?"

Mario leaned forward, "Even The Alliance makes mistakes. There are people that were burned by Steiner, people that want revenge.

We just have to find them. And when we do we will have the extra ammunition we need."

"Do you really think that we will find someone that will openly go against The Alliance?"

"Yes, I do. We just have to find that right ones."

Mario's determination inspired Karen. She had been trying to take out The Alliance alone for so long that is was nice to have an ally.

"Ok, so what is the plan? Why are we going to Texas?"

"Because that is where one of my trusted contacts live. And there we can get supplies."

"Ok, let's get started."

The two strategized until dawn. When they were ready to leave and head for Texas, Mario paused and asked Karen, "I need to know here and now, without a shadow of a doubt, you with me. No backing down. Once we start this we won't have a choice. We either bring down The Alliance or we will die at their hand."

Karen grabbed Mario's hand.

Her palm was warm. She locked her eyes with his and replied, "No backing down."

Mario squeezed her hand in his and said, "Ok. Let's go."

Chapter Five

Judson Steiner calmly tapped his pen on his mahogany desk.

This will end soon.

He stood and walked around his plush office, mauling over in his mind recent events.

Judson's secretary, Angelica Jones walked into his office.

"Sir, here are the files you requested."

"Oh, yes, put them anywhere."

Angelica did as she was told and was about to return to her own desk.

"Ms. Jones."

"Yes, sir?"

"Do you like it here?"

Angelica was puzzled but not surprised. Judson liked mystery and putting people on the spot.

"Sir?"

"Do you like working for me?"

"Do you like your job?"

Angelica felt heat rush to her cheeks. Judson made her feel intimidated. He had a presence that made her feel small. And even now he seemed sleek and commanding.

"Yes sir, very much."

"Hmm."

Not sure if she was to be excused Angelica asked, " Mr. Steiner is that all?"

Judson was leaning back in his leather chair behind his desk.

"Mr. Steiner."

"Oh, yes, of course. That is all Ms. Jones."

Judson stood and paced around his desk, then gazed out the office window over the city.

No one leaves The Alliance. No one.

Walking back to his desk he pushed a button that alerted Angelica.

"Yes, Mr. Steiner."

"Make a lunch appointment with Brett Stevens for today at my usual place."

"Yes sir."

A few hours later Brett found himself seated at an elegant table. Judson had not arrived yet.

Brett already knew why he was called to this lunch. He had failed. Mario Valdez and Karen Briscoe were both rogue.

He didn't know Karen but he did know Mario. He trusted him.

And that is what was fueling his rage.

Judson arrived and sat across from Brett. A waiter now stood to the left of Judson.

"Mr. Steiner so good to see you again sir. Will you be having your usual choice?"

"Yes, and my colleague will have the same."

"Very good sir."

"I hope you like lamb, Brett."

He did not but knew better than to announce this fact.

"That will be fine sir."

"Let's get down to business. I am sure you know why I called this meeting."

"I do."

"And what are you doing about our situation."

"We are closing in. I trained him and so I know how he thinks, where he will go."

Judson eyed him.

Brett waited, a bit anxious.

He knew Judson was powerful and always got what he wanted.

Judson was now tapping his index finger on the table.

"Brett, have I told you about the agent that had your position before you joined us?"

"No, you have not."

"Before you joined The Alliance, there was a man, Angelo, who ran my training department. He was good, very good. He had connections that I did not have. In fact a lot of our funding and support is due to the relationships Angelo built for The Alliance."

Brett sat quietly, wondering what happened to Angelo if so much thanks on The Alliance's part was due him.

"But Angelo got greedy. He tried to steal the company from me. Back in those days, I was a lot more, shall I say, hands-on.

I had to get involved and resolve the matter."

Judson gave Brett a cold stare and continued, "I don't like getting involved."

Brett had worked for Judson long enough to know he liked metaphors and that when he used them there was always a point he was getting across.

"I understand, sir. You will not have to interject yourself in this situation. It is being handled."

"Good."

The waiter had now returned to the table and placed a beautiful meal in front of both men.

Judson smiled his sleek smile and said, "Bon appetit."

Chapter Six

Mario stared ahead at the pavement as he drove down the interstate.

Karen was sleeping in the passenger seat and seemed to be peaceful.

Poor thing. She had it rough the last few years.

Karen moved around the seat, still asleep, but trying to get comfortable.

Mario wasn't sure what was in the future for either one of them.

He worried for Karen. He wasn't that much older than her but he felt his life was spent. His mother had already passed away and he lost touch with his sister years ago.

I have lived my life. Her's is just beginning. And to have this burden. No one should have to be in this predicament.

Karen rubbed her eyes and began to wake up.

"Where are we?"

"Just outside of Amarillo."

She took in the surroundings.

It was a lot different than she imagined. The land was flat, and had a wildness to it. Even though they were going right through town she felt like there was a piece of this prairie land that was free. She liked it.

"So, when do we stop?"

"We are going a few miles outside of town to my contact's ranch. He is expecting us."

Nothing was said for the next hour. The two were deep in their own thoughts.

Mario turned on a dirt road and drove another ten miles. Then he turned left down a long and narrow driveway. There was a house nestled back from the road.

To Karen it seemed it was a distant world. She liked Texas. She envisioned what her life would be like on a ranch, with a husband and family of her own. She shot a glance at Mario. She blushed a bit at the thought that entered her mind, that he could be her husband someday.

You are being silly. The adrenaline of the last few days have clouded your judgment. He is a colleague and we are working a mission together, nothing more.

They were now parked in front of the ranch house. Mario turned the engine off and said, "You are going to like Clive."

Once out of the truck, Karen saw an old cowboy walking out of the house to meet them.

"Mario! You are a sight for sore eyes!" The men gave each other an hardly hug.

"And who is this?" Clive questioned with a smile.

Karen did like him. He was genuine.

Karen went to shake Clive's hand, "I am Karen Briscoe."

"Nice to meet you, little lady."

"How about we all go inside and I pour us a glass of sweet tea. Then y'all can tell me what brings you out to this part of the world."

Karen followed Mario and Clive inside. She wished they could stay outside and breath in the evening air. But she knew indoors was safer.

Clive showed them to a small dining room table and offered them both a seat.

"Y'all sit down and I will get the glasses and tea."

Once Clive was out of the room Karen whispered, "You didn't tell him we were coming?"

Mario shook his head, "Too risky. I don't think The Alliance knows about Clive but I couldn't be too sure."

Karen understood Mario's caution.

"Here we are." Clive said as he handed Karen her tea, then Mario his.

Clive sat across from Mario and next to Karen.

"Ok, Mario, what's this all about?"

Karen sipped her tea, which she thought was the best tea she had ever drank, and waiting for Mario's response.

"We left The Alliance."

Clive sat motionless. Karen wondered if he had heard what Mario said.

"We are not just leaving but we are wanting to take them out."

"We plan on going into Steiner's office, and from there we will hack into his computer and get the files we need to take him down."

Again Clive said nothing.

Karen was beginning to think this might have been a mistake.

What if Clive has double-crossed Mario and he plans to turn us in.

Finally, Clive spoke. "It's about time."

Karen surprised, looked at Clive. His gentle smile crossed his face and he patted her hand. "Don't you worry little lady. I have known ole Mario here for a while now. He contacted me when he decided to be a double agent. He found my file one day and took the chance that I might not be so loyal to The Alliance."

Karen now not able to contain her curiosity, asked, "What happened?"

Clive pointed to a framed photograph sitting on a hutch in the corner of the room.

"That is my Annie."

Karen saw that the picture was of a beautiful woman that looked to be around forty. She had long golden blond hair and was smiling.

"The Alliance wanted to buy this ranch. Judson Steiner was willing to pay a bundle for it. Even paid me a visit himself. I admit he was offering more than it was worth. But my Annie." Clive's voice cracked. He composed himself.

"My Annie, she loved this place and she didn't want to sell. So I told him, no sir, it's not for sale."

Karen spoke, "I imagine that didn't set well with Judson."

"No, ma'am it sure didn't."

Clive's eyes were misting over and he continued, "They say it was a car accident in town. There was even witnesses that say, Annie ran a red light and the truck driver had no way of stopping."

Clive pulled out his handker-chief from his jean pocket and wiped his eyes.

"But I know better." Now Clive's face was stern.

"The other driver supposedly died in that crash too. So, I never got the chance to ask him what exactly happened. But I know. I know."

Karen's own eyes were glassing over now. It was these kind of assignments she knew far too well.

Someone that dared to challenge The Alliance was eliminated. Judson took each challenge as a personal attack. As if these people were challenging him. And he made sure they paid for it.

Mario now spoke, "So, it is time for restitution. We need supplies if we want this mission to work."

Clive grinned that charming smile again, "Well, sir, you came to the right place."

He led Mario and Karen to the back yard and to a cellar. Inside it looked like and ordinary root cellar. There was some canned vegetables, jellies and jams on the wooden shelves that lined the walls. Clive spun one of the jars and the shelf opened, leading to another room.

Karen couldn't help but feel excitement, "That was awesome."

Now in a completely different room the three of them were looking at weapons, communication devices, bullet-proof vests, any-thing and everything that they would need on their mission.

Mario already had a duffel bag in hand and was filling it with supplies.

Karen asked, "How can we ever repay you for your help?"

With a cold stare Clive answered, "Bring them down."

Chapter Seven

Mario and Karen were back on the road. She was sad to leave.

One thing was certain, she made a new friend and she would be back.

The miles and hours stretched on. They only stopped for fuel and used that time to get a snack, and use the restroom. Then it was back on the road.

While on the highway, Karen was lost in her thoughts about Mario. She felt safe with him. She hadn't felt safe in years.

Karen's thoughts were interrupted, the pick-up shook with a thud.

The back of their rig was fish-tailing. Someone had hit them from behind.

"We have been hit!" Mario shouted.

"Take the wheel!" He directed Karen. She did as he commanded. He turned in the seat and grabbed the duffel bag that he had thrown in the back.

Within seconds Mario was steering the wheel again and giving Karen orders.

"Get the guns out!" Quickly she had two guns in hand, loaded and ready. She handed one to Mario and kept one for herself.

As the pick-up sped down the highway, a gray Ford Explorer was gaining on them.

"They are coming up fast!"

Karen aimed and fired a shot that went through the back window of the pick-up and blazed towards the Explorer. She was a good shot and hit her target, the driver.

Mario kept his foot on the accelerator and the SUV behind them was spinning out of control.

Soon it hit a guardrail, flipped three times and then exploded.

"Do you think it was Brett?" Karen asked breathless.

"No, I think it was one of his agents. Brett doesn't want to do the hands on stuff, if he can help it. But he will probably get involved now."

"Since we are still alive?" Karen asked quickly.

"Yes."

Mario was impressed by Karen's shooting skills. Plus, she could keep her composure during the heat of an assignment. Even though his mind was telling him his feelings were due to the adrenaline that pumped through his veins, his heart was telling him that he was falling in love with Karen.

Love is not an option.

Mario had no idea that Karen was beginning to feel towards him what he felt for her.

We work well together.

Neither of them spoke. Both kept a watchful eye on the road ahead.

At 2:00 a.m. Mario pulled into a mom and pop dinner that was open 24-hours.

"We need to eat and to change up our plan a bit."

Karen knew he was right and as much as she hated to get off the road she welcomed a hot meal.

The diner was a classic 50s decor. The food was an all-American menu and it smelled delicious.

Mario ordered a hamburger and fries while Karen ordered a chicken basket.

There was a elderly man sitting in a booth across from them. But other than him, they had the place to themselves.

Karen dipped a couple of fries in ketchup, "What do we do now?"

Mario had just bitten into his cheese burger and answered her question as he chewed.

"We knew we would have an altercation along the way. So, we still head to New York but we just change up the route. Take a few back roads."

She liked the idea. She also liked that Mario didn't get rattled under pressure. She knew he had been an agent with The Alliance for a long time but he also had been out of the field for a while. She wondered if he might be a bit rusty. Today's events proved he was still on top of his game.

"A piece of paper." Karen said.

"What?"

"You asked me what made me want to leave The Alliance. It started with a piece of paper."

Chapter Eight

Six Years Earlier

Karen walked into her favorite coffee shop and sat at in her regular spot. Every day she bought a white chocolate breve.

But after a big assignment she treated herself to a double hazelnut latte.

Today was a latte day.

Sitting at the corner table she looked inside the coffee cup. The beverage was steaming with heat. She blew it softly and took a sip.

Delicious.

Karen liked this particular table because she could watch the traffic outside the window.

Taking another sip of coffee, she saw on the table a small pamphlet.

She scanned the room to see if anyone was watching her. Working for The Alliance made her paranoid.

It is just a piece of paper. Don't be ridiculous.

Quietly, she read the booklet.

At first she scoffed at it's contents. It was clear and to the point. A simple message about Jesus, Heaven and Hell.

She flipped it to the other side of the table.

If I knew who laid this here I would give them a piece of my mind!

Karen tried to forget the paper. She looked out the window.

Her eyes went back to the pamphlet.

Grabbing up the paper she mumbled under her breath, "This is so stupid."

She was about to throw it in the trash when she noticed a name on the back.

Calvary Baptist Church.

She read the address, it was only a couple of blocks from the coffee shop.

Maybe I should go down there and tell them I don't want to be bothered with their literature.

Karen, gathered her things and headed for the door.

She was still not sure if she should go by the church or just let the matter drop.

It couldn't hurt to drive by.

In a couple of minutes Karen was in front of a beautiful, modest bricked building.

She sat in the parking, thinking.

I guess I could go in and take a look around.

The front door was unlocked. Karen let herself inside.

"Hello?"

She walked down a small hallway.

"May I help you?"

There was a middle-aged woman standing behind her. She was thin and short but pretty. She had brown hair that she had pulled back into a pony-tail.

"Hi."

Suddenly, all of Karen's courage and angry faded. This lady had a kind face. She felt awkward standing there.

"Is there something I can help you with?"

"Well, I guess so. I read this paper at the coffee shop a couple of blocks from here and it had this church address on it."

"Oh, yes of course. I am happy to answer any of your questions."

Karen couldn't think of anything. All she wanted to say before seemed pointless now.

The woman was talking again.

"I can show you some scriptures in the Bible."

Karen surprised herself when she agreed to look in the Bible with this lady.

Time went by quickly. She learned that the woman's name was Jill Hardy. In her youth she was addicted to drugs and had been in out of jail.

"If it wasn't for the Lord I would probably be dead."

Karen was staring at her, blankly. She didn't know how to process everything Jill had said.

"It just sounds too simple." Karen finally replied.

" I know. I thought the same thing. But it really is simple. I already knew I was bad, nobody had to convince me of that. But I couldn't believe that someone so perfect and so holy could love me enough to die for me. That someone so good would want me to have a home with Him in Heaven."

Karen understood exactly. She was a logical person. She didn't get caught up in dramatic emotions. This fact helped her in many assignments. So, when it came to matters of the heart, she had difficulty.

"You think on it. Here is my number, call me anytime."

Karen took the paper Jill handed her.

"Thank you."

Karen sat in her car, turned the ignition and put the car in reverse. It was almost like she was on autopilot.

Could it be that easy? Jill seemed so, genuine.

That night at home, Karen was still thinking about the day's events.

I never met someone so sincere. She really believes what she is saying.

Karen still had the small pamphlet that brought her to Jill. She read it over and over.

The words printed on that paper were striking a chord in her heart.

Exhausted, she went to bed and drifted off to sleep.

That night she had a dream.

She couldn't remember it's details but she did remembered how it made her feel. She wanted what Jill had, peace.

At 5:00 a.m. Karen was sitting in her bed,quiet.

She wasn't sure what to say, or how to say it. She wasn't the type of person that prayed.

God, I know you can hear me, I am not sure how to start. I am pretty sure you already know what has gone on these last couple of days.

She stopped for a moment. She felt foolish, like a little child.

But she recalled something she heard as a young girl. *The faith of a child.*

Her neighbor had been talking to her mother, and she made that statement, the faith of a child.

Karen couldn't remember why or what they were talking about but like a flash those words were in her mind.

M*aybe that is what it takes a child-like faith.*

Karen thought of assignments she had successfully done over the last couple months. For the first time she felt, guilt.

God, I know I am not a good person. You are good, and perfect.

Jill told me how You took my punishment on Yourself. I ask for forgiveness, and I ask that I can go to Heaven.

Karen was now crying, and she was a little surprised. She wasn't accustomed to feeling such raw emotions. She ended her prayer with, *I ask You to save me.*

She remained quiet for the next few moments. She received what she was longing for, peace.

Chapter Nine

Present Day

Karen told Mario the whole story, about Jill, the paper, everything. She also told him that she tried to stay with The Alliance and change the company from the inside. That wouldn't work. Finally, she couldn't do the assignments anymore. She had to leave.

Once she was finished she waited to see Mario's reaction. He was thinking.

"Well, that is a good reason to leave." he commented, with a grin.

Karen smiled, and took a bite of her chicken.

It was the first time Mario had seen her smile. It was a nice.

He wished he could make her smile everyday.

"Ok, we need to get back on the road."

"Yep."

Karen offered to drive for a while. Mario hesitated but knew he was getting tired.

"Maybe just for a few hours." Mario slept and Karen drove.

The next day Mario heard Karen's voice, saying, "Wake up, sleepy head."

He rubbed his eyes. "Where are we?"

"Just a couple of hours outside of New York City."

Mario was surprised.

"Whoa, how long did I sleep?"

"I let you sleep as long as you needed."

Mario felt refreshed. He was thankful Karen did allow him to sleep.

"You ready for this?"

"As ready as I will ever be."

The plan was set. Mario and Karen both were on point. Since Mario was more recognizable than Karen he would work the outside of the building. He would be in charge of getting Karen in and out of the building and keeping communication.

The final step before going into The Alliance was getting themselves into character.

Karen stopped at run down motel about an hour outside the city limits. It was the kind of place they didn't ask a lot questions. Especially, when you pay in cash.

Once in their room they went to work.

Karen took a box of hair dye into the bathroom with her. She was going from soft auburn hair to black. She looked at her reflect- ion in the mirror.

Here we go.

After Karen had her hair dowsed in hair color, she sat on a chair across from Mario.

"What are you working on?"

Mario showed Karen her guest pass.

"So you can get into The Alliance."

That was the plan, Karen would be a potential client there for an interview with Judson.

Karen held the card in her hand. "This looks great."

"Thanks. I just hope Judson hasn't changed his system."

Karen was worried about that too. Most of The Alliance was very cutting edge with technology. But to their advantage Judson would keep an old-school approach to certain areas of the company. He liked having the control. And because of this, the guest passes were not electronic but were give in the old fashioned way, paper and ink. That made getting into The Alliance easier for Karen.

"Time to wash this stuff out of my hair." Karen got up and picked up her backpack filled with clothes. She washed her hair, got dressed, and came out into the main room.

Mario was now changed in to his outfit as well. He was dressed as a road construction worker.

He noticed Karen when she walked into the room.

She was stunning. Her hair now dark but still pretty was shaped in a neat bun on the back of her head. She was wearing glasses, a straight tan skirt with a red blouse and red pumps.

"Wow!" Mario exclaimed.

Karen looked at her skirt then her shoes, "Is something wrong."

"No, not all." Mario said trying to recompose himself.

"You really look the part. You did a great job on your disguise."

"Thank you. It's not too much?"

"No, not too much." Mario stared a moment and then replied, "I think we are ready. Now we just need a van."

"I saw one behind the motel office." Announced Karen.

"Then that is our ride." said Mario.

The two crept to the back of the motel, the van was still there.

In the back of the van they loaded up the gear Clive had given them. Then Mario hopped in the driver's seat.

He fumbled with some wires and in a few minutes the van was running.

Back on the road, they were now going to The Alliance. Karen felt a surge of nerves pulsate through her body. *This is it.*

Mario looked at her from the peripheral of his right eye.

"You ok?"

"Yeah, just getting all the nervousness out now. I can't go in there jittery."

Mario patted Karen's arm.

"You are going to do great."

Karen shook her head in the affirmative. She breathed in slowly, through her nose, and released her air through her mouth.

With in the hour, they were two blocks east of The Alliance.

"I will be with you the whole time." Mario promised as he handed Karen her ear piece.

"I know. I am ready."

Mario was now in the back of the van and Karen was walking towards The Alliance.

"I am approaching the lobby doors."

Once inside Karen was all about business. She knew if she showed any hesitance, any anxiety the mission would be blown.

In the middle of the lobby was a check in station. She walked up to the two uniformed men sitting behind the desk.

"I have an appointment with Mr. Steiner." Karen said flatly as she handed them her guest pass.

One of the security guards was young and cheerful. The other guard was older and serious.

"You will be going to the tenth floor. Elevators are down the hall and to the right."

Karen thanked the men as they handed the guest pass back to her.

"I am in."

"Good. If our timing is right and Judson is still a creature of habit, he will be gone on his lunch break."

"We are taking a lot of chances here."

Mario agreed. "We have too. We have no inside man. I know Judson.

He is structured and likes order and control."

Karen now riding in the elevator, found the soft background music amusing.

The doors opened and she was in the hub of The Alliance.

Cubicles and small offices filled the large area, and in each space there was an Alliance agent hard at work.

No one noticed her. She walked to the side of the room and down a small narrow hallway. This led to Judson's office. She was preparing for her encounter with his secretary. She would not have an appointment on her schedule.

Maybe she will be at lunch too. While this thought entered her mind, she turned the last corner before Judson's office.

She stopped. Angelica Jones sat at her desk, looking at a computer screen and biting into a ham sandwich.

Karen slipped backwards around the corner. She knew the woman.

"We might have a small problem." Karen informed Mario.

"What's wrong?"

"The secretary. I know her. We used to do clerical work together."

"Do you think she will recognize you?"

" I am not sure. We were three cubicles from each other. I promoted to agent and never knew what became of her." Karen peeked around the corner.

"I guess now I know."

"What do you want to do?"

Mario quipped.

Karen remembered the promise she and Mario had made when they first agreed to work together.

"No backing down. I am going in."

"Be careful."

Karen turned the corner and approached Angelica's desk. Still looking at her computer screen, Angelica questioned, "May I help you?"

"I am here to see Mr. Steiner."

" I am sorry he is at lunch."

Angelica replied, while turning her chair to face Karen. Their eyes met. Karen knew. She recognized her.

Neither said anything. Karen was strategizing what she should do next. Angelica was a sweet lady, but she wasn't going to let her stand in her way. Not when she was so close.

Just when Karen was about to make a move, Angelica spoke.

"You have five minutes. Then I call security."

Karen wasn't expecting this act of kindness.

"Thank you."

Karen sat behind Judson's desk and was now in front of his computer.

"I am in."

"Good job! Ok, let me work my magic, and I will have his password for you."

Mario keyed quickly on a hand held keyboard and then chuckled.

"The password is, domination."

Karen rolled her eyes, "That sounds about right."

She was in Judson's files and scanned through different titles.

Nothing looked too promising, until Karen saw the numbers, 589.

Gottcha!

The number was a code that the agents used in communications. It meant eliminate the target.

Karen put in a chip and downloaded the file.

Three minutes left.

She was about to close out the computer when at the bottom of file 589 she saw the words "Briscoe Estate."

She clicked it open. There in black and white was all the information about her parents.

They had died when Karen was in her last semester of college. She still remembered Amy's voice on the phone, how it cracked when she told her that their parents had died in a plane crash.

Karen felt her head starting to spin, her throat was closing.

An asthma attack was coming on, she wanted to stop breathing, not fight it, but just stop breathing.

I can't…I can't give up.

If I do they will have died in vain.

She sat still, taking in deep breaths. At first they were unsteady and quick. Then she calmed herself to even deep breaths.

She left Judson's office, Angelica was no where to be found. Karen took the stairs and went out the maintenance door.

"I am out and heading towards you now."

"Copy that."

Karen's paced quickened. She wanted to be in the van with Mario, she wanted to feel safe.

Once with him she could let go of the emotions, tell him that The Alliance murdered her parents.

She went down a side-alley and was one block from the van.

Almost there.

A woman stepped in front of her with a gun pointed at her chest. "Hey there big sis."

Karen startled, took a step backwards. In a whisper she said, "Amy?"

"Yeah, that's right. Little sister is all grown up. And you big sis, well you are one hard person to track down."

"How is this possible?"

"Do you mean how do I work for The Alliance? Oh, yeah, that is your fault."

Karen's chest was tightening.

"How is it my fault? I was trying to protect you!"

"By leaving me!" Amy screamed.

"You were all I had and you left me." Amy took a step towards Karen, still aiming the gun on her.

"So, they recruited me.

Joining The Alliance was the best decision I ever made. And as luck would have it, I was assigned to find you."

"Angelica." Karen realized.

"Yes, Angelica called in the tip that you were in the building.

Stupid mistake, Karen. You wanted out so bad and now you will have Judson to contend with." Amy stepped closer to Karen.

"Or maybe I will just do it myself."

"Amy, you don't know the truth, The Alliance, Judson, he killed our parents."

Amy's stance weakened for a moment. Then with more vigor she straightened and yelled, "Lies! You are a liar!"

"No I am not, Amy. I have the proof."

Before Karen could say any-more, she heard a familiar voice, "Drop the weapon."

Amy turned and shot at Mario and then ran between two buildings and was gone.

Karen raced to Mario.

"Have you been hit?"

"No, she missed. We've been blown I see."

"It's much worse. That was my sister. The Alliance has gotten to her. And they killed my parents."

Karen was no longer able to control her sobs. Mario held her close and whispered words of comfort.

Finally, Karen was able to stop her tears. "I am sorry. We don't need this right now."

"Don't worry about it. That is what partners are for."

Karen smiled, "I guess we are partners now."

"So, what do we do now?" Mario challenged. He understood that the situation had changed for her.

"What do you want to do?" he asked.

Karen thought of her parents and how much she truly missed them. She felt remorse for all the targets she had taken out herself.

Now she understood how the families of the victims felt. She wanted to help her sister and she knew the only way to do that was to expose The Alliance.

"I want to get back to the van, regroup, and take down The Alliance."

Mario, impressed by her drive replied, "Then that is exactly what we will do."